ALMOST SATORI

ALMOST SATORI

mokradi

Storigin Publishing

ISBN: 978-1-7776826-3-7

Concept by mokradi
Illustrations and cover design by Tyler Dail

mokradi_

for
the one
in us all

CONTENTS

Mother this period of quarantine, I was to use as time sent from heavens to aid in the expansion of mind, I am afraid, I have taken far too seriously, for today I lost all of my boundaries, seeing thoughts very literally, oozing out my ears, falling as drops down to the ground, watering the earth, which reclaimed my planted spine, mother, I could not tell my flesh from my soil.

This expansion I was after, an awakening that belonged to me, I could not find…

Oh such tears of joy, pray, on the losing of a mind.

Umbilical

Mother's comb parted with me across oceans

a new strand,

inherited split-ends.

Introverted since birth,

I see the world in silence.

Everyone chasing their dreams, in a rush

efforts to speak them into existence.

But me? I do not talk much.

Awkward nature, maybe I was born like this

Ma face timing, asking me about my days

my face unfazed, so much to say…

but these emotions are stuck in my throat,

afraid of its journey

through all this space

between us.

I can jump

from this moment here to points in my past

out-of-body experiences, to master the art

of letting go.

Monsoon rain would flood the village with elated children

no school, out in the playgrounds barefoot!

We returned home in the evening

to limitless skies of neon pink.

Exhausted with laughter, we fell asleep

heels still clinging to caked mud.

A road

on which God and man travel,

one set of footprints.

A diversity of faces, bodies in continuous osmosis

hurrying to work downtown - a splendid illusion.

A step may stretch the road.

These days, I wait for doors to open

instead of kicking them down.

You can always force yourself in,

but be at peace where you don't belong?

The red and white

striped shirt

you ironed for me

when I left the motherland

is still here with me,

with your folds in place

I'm afraid,

to take it out

in case, it erase

the creases you made,

like the bumps

of our shared memories

which, with each day

keep flattening.

I want to say

I love you, Ma.

The words in my stomach move their way up

just to get stuck behind the tongue,

where did I pick this up from?

A precondition from past generations still remains undiagnosed.

This is where I let go

this is where the road becomes a V,

parts into two and we are forced to choose.

This is where I choose to let go.

A lack of ambition is good,

this will not be taught in schools.

For in a world built of incentives,

without a goal what is a man to do?

Live in silence, without thought, it is not:

a wasting of days,

a killing of weeks,

a consuming of time. You fool.

Instead, pray, let the time consume you.

Family gossip,

the cousin back home has twins on the way

a new house purchased - last summer was the housewarming.

This summer,

the nursery under the roof

has heat coming through - the house warming.

Get busy,

building cradles for a past yet to arrive

as Atrahasis, Noah, and Manu - before water broke the warning.

Here, on the other side of the Earth

the Sun casts a frozen shadow.

Searching for soap, I leave the first-world tap open.

Warm water flowing over my skin

is a privilege I steal

from the bodies

of my grandchildren.

A mother tongue speaks in transgenerational trauma

of inherited negligence,

where children tested in exams

had their fingers wrapped up in bandages.

Toppers, we called them, were fluent in numbers

but untutored in any of the five languages.

So, joint families broke in silence

for money spoke when brothers couldn't.

Insecure,

when others do well.

When others rise up

it feels like I fall down.

A state of mind-conditioned,

the perils of being raised brown.

You will find it necessary

to let things go

for the simple reason,

your hands need to be empty to receive.

                              But the things I have

                                    are hard to let go

                                    the things I want,

                                    I want them more.

                          So let me go when the time comes

I am holding onto more things than my arms can hold.

                          For a brief moment, I'll have it all

                                  a split second,

                              but for that split second,

                                    I am glorious.

Inhaled too much, unstable walking, thoughts passing…

As a rule of thumb,

I know it's too much

when these thoughts start to slow,

and just before forgetting it all

I see the distance between each thought grow.

Trauma turned into a thief,

I am not sure what it stole.

Searched everywhere within,

but I don't seem to have it anymore.

Born in captivity, I am still a prisoner to my habits:

a rush of blood,

for proof of love.

To calm this rage
I sink through the bathtub.

Water heavy

drifting off…

Wonder on valium nights,

what do the caged whales dream of?

-    valium whales

A head filled with morning mist,

from last night's bad decisions.

Mind throbbing, as the heart

pushes itself out the arteries.

Efforts to unify both, in grandiose hopes

of ending all these made-up divisions.

There are seasons within you,

rhythms of creation

and decimation.

Like spring that ushers in the green,

falls soon after when the grey skies bleed.

You were growing so much last year,

now begins your self-destructive streak.

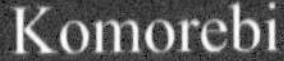

Komorebi

Dappled sunlight

through moving branches.

My discipline.

-    komorebi

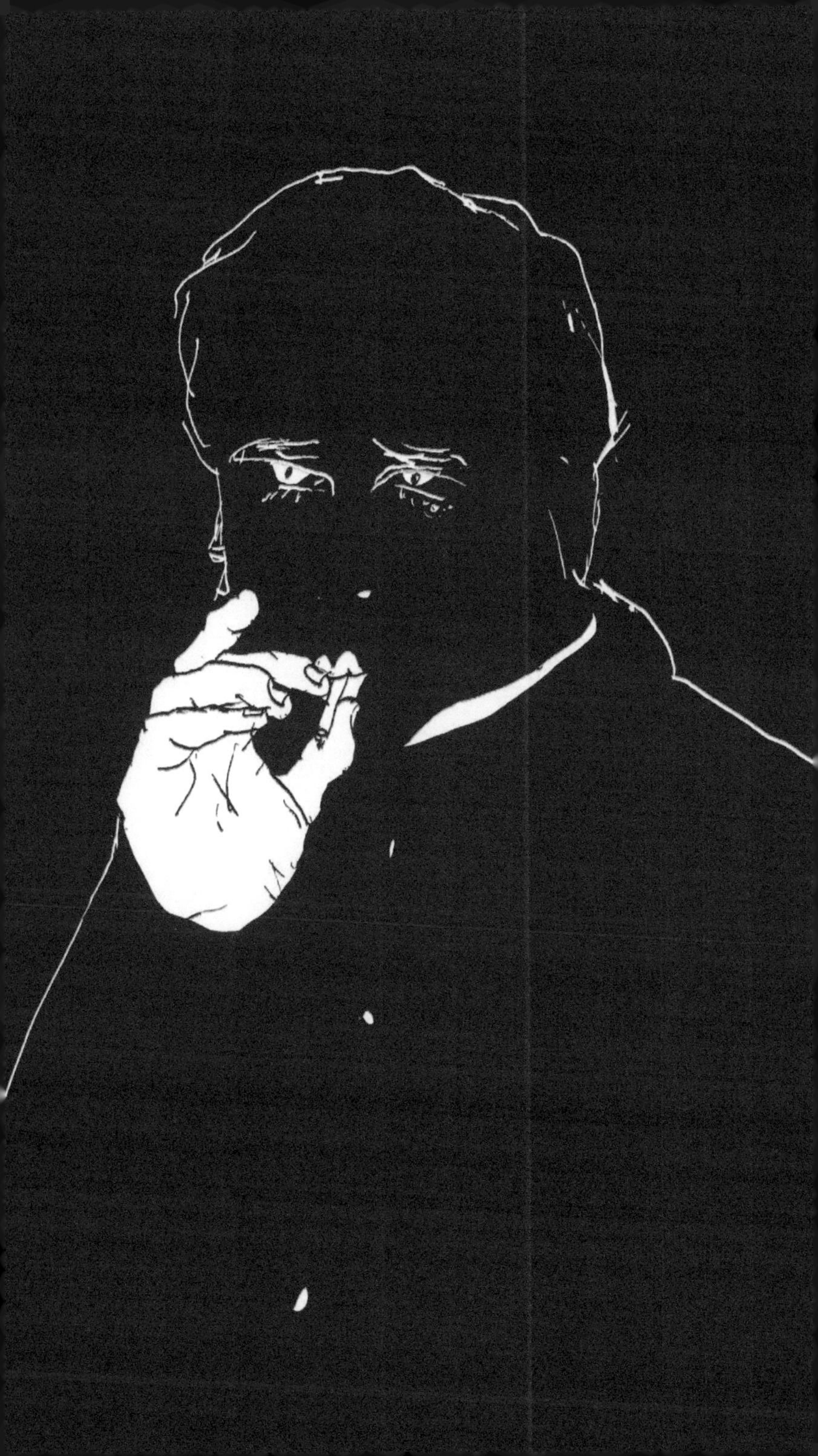

You've stopped painting on instinct

a prey to the world's opinion, I see your heart sinking.

It's fine, it takes time

before he stopped listening, Van Gogh too was once Vincent.

Blood-brain barrier broken

rapid uptake

across membranes

to escape memories

in grey cells and other

troubled spaces

reaching inner zen

in false pursuits of meeting Buddha

on the road, two grams, in flames

set fire to the laws of attraction,

I have stopped attracting

let me float for a while

like a raft, directionless

until the Universe tugs me in rescue

having finally accepted

my SOS.

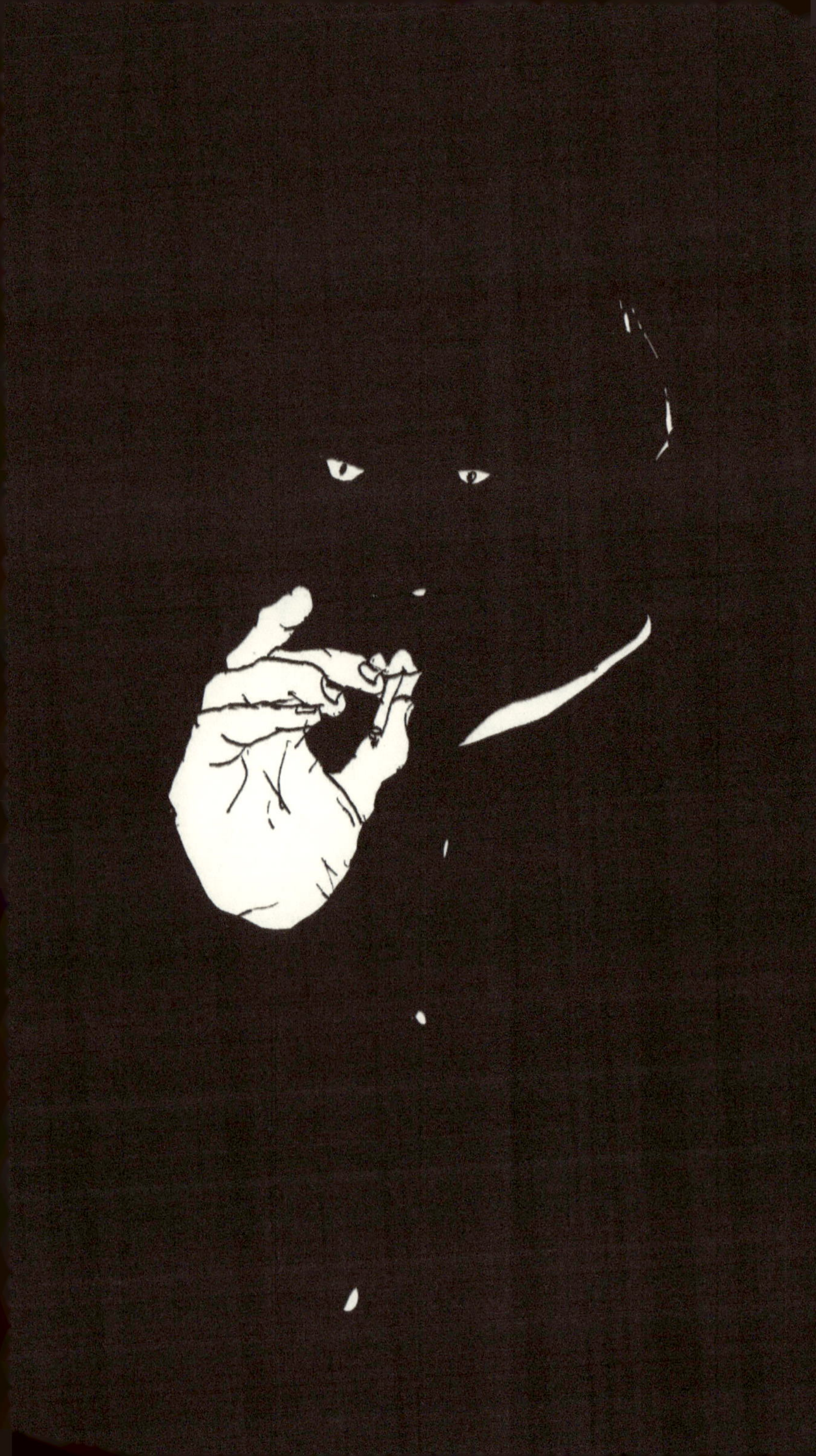

No visibility,

December air is still in silence.

The mountains in the distance - I cannot see.

But the ski lights on their surface,

glitter like a cluster of diamonds.

Divine lights beckon,

as greed goes to bed with dreams of breaking into heavens.

Memories with you

walking down Roman avenues

big promises, under bigger edifices

not sure if we followed through?

For my past lifetime, in bits, resurfaces

and the rest of our dreams are forgotten,

somewhere in these ancient Universes.

Images of a past life

flicker through in burst lights,

reincarnations are common

but suppressed in the West side…

Friends I laughed with, had oiled hair

sweaty foreheads, and wore white layers

in a Summer's world, filled with golden warmth

you will not find today.

Whirlwind from this bourbon

in my sheets, as the bed spins

battling demons, it goes both ways.

It's okay, I say

for when I lose, I win

but when I win, it feels the same.

A mind mending things

it knows, it will break tomorrow.

Human consciousness,

the precious gift in this life and the next.

Such a shame that the lessons I've learned in this life,

will slip away in death.

After rebirth,

I shall have to unlearn them all over again.

Sound Meditation

She said you should think twice

before walking out,

I left without listening.

Now, in my head her silence echoes

deafening.

House plants grow

green moss on walls,

brown roots crawl over marble floors.

Like Rama in Dandaka,

I try to carve out forests

to keep with me what's honest

lost it; Sealed somewhere inside this concrete soul.

m o k r a d i

Back into that space

where everything I see, looks fake

universal realities or your Instagram page

consume me in cursed energies.

Last life I was a sage, performing rituals

yet not knowing how to pray.

Your actions shall reveal how much you care

for action is love and love, the highest form of prayer.

A tension in you,

asked for attention on you - that I failed to pay.

Am I having second thoughts?
I pled the fifth.

The second was a long time back, since then
I've had third, fourth and fifth.

Be careful with the promises you make

for the same person, you will not be

when the time comes

for these promises to break.

If I were to die

from a tumor of the mind

my thoughts would multiply

on all the things I could never buy you

even time.

Your words fell softly like rain

washing away my faults,

the sound of thunder

could never do the same.

Expression and silence

are like yin

and yin.

I know

I am not the master of myself,

in this play of cosmic love and words, unsaid

but sometimes this knowledge is what makes me go rage

lifetimes of imprisonment, liberation awaits.

Back then, he don't talk much

for he don't know a lot.

Now he know so much,

but even more so now,

he don't talk.

-    the poet's trouble 1

Everyone had ideas of him

pierced-in perceptions

close to real, but never really real.

That's why he stayed in his head

away from the pain,

from all the pretense

this new world dictates

on us, for which

he was never made.

-    the poet's trouble 2

Self-destructive habits of greatness

the poet, one night, by candle side

to describe the Sun, took flight

so he could learn, before he could write

but the heart wanted to feel,

to drink the ink before the ink sinked in

all poisons kill,

but they can only poison from within.

In attempts to be more intimate

before his wings of wax melted,

the poet flew into the light.

-      the poet's trouble 3

The only way to heal pain

is to feel it again and then release it

to feel it again and then release it

pulsating back and forth,

over and over, till it's gone.

Miracles too, are birthed from such pain

like you when born.

March trees are still naked,

an arabesque of branches outstretched

with open arms to receive.

A furious afternoon of relentless drizzle

yields a wine-red evening,

brimming with silence.

A sparrow ventures out alone.

Your puppet for tonight, these drinks loosen.

Revealing traits

in your back-laced dress, your dance steps.

DNA untying,

strings that make a human.

Brown skin,

she has stripes on her thigh

marks like a tiger, fight in a world

where the lion is king.

Tearing open an orange tangerine,

juices ooze out and lick my sticky thumbs.

Show me a civilized way of tasting nectars.

The space around us

was heavy with stillness.

A presence, we could feel

but chose not to name it.

The three am streets

belong to lovers and addicts.

Ambulance sirens respond

to overdose calls every half an hour.

We fall asleep to grown-up lullabies.

Mountains were Mountains

I am growing a space of nurture within myself

that I can take you to, on days you don't feel like yourself.

mokradi

Don't miss me too much,

for I have missed me too

only by a few seconds, but enough time

for this me to come through.

-    I don't need love, I am love.

Life imitates art

so I imitate life

write quickly or you miss it,

and there goes the rest of your life.

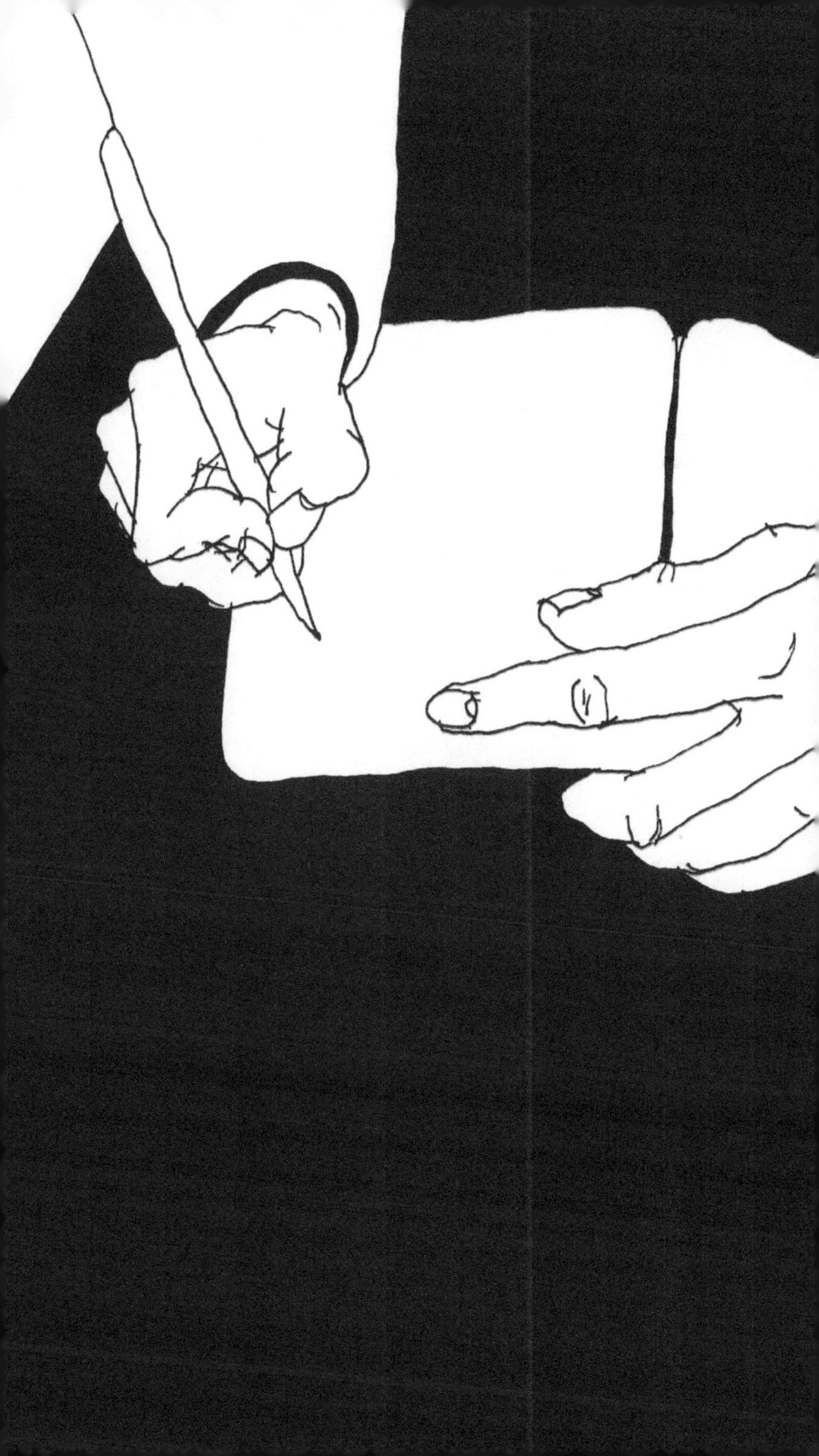

In Your devotion,

this pen writes itself.

No offerings or prayers

can bribe You into revealing

what has already been written.

Finding potential

is likely to

deplete it.

- an afternoon (almost) satori.

Early morning chanting,

the Lord's light, illuminates my veins

making my red blood cells swim,

sustained energies in arteries

replaces a thirst for nicotine.

I soak in the sun

I soak in your words

I soak in your songs

till I'm full

with the four corners of the world's Love.

For too long,

I've been selling my soul

to the wrong ones.

Now I know,

to sell it so to God alone,

Who buys it with smiles

paying in gold

for a life He knew

was His all along.

A calm vacuous space

somehow overspilling with extreme energy,

ecstatic tranquility.

Vibrations swinging back and forth

so fast that it appears

absolutely still.

Experiments with my experience

looking to Source inside for deliverance.

I realize the act of searching

is itself the idea that imprisons us.

The evidence is in the experience.

The evidence is the experience.

The experience is the evidence.

When I write, people think

I write from a place somewhere deep within.

The truth is

when I write, it seems like

I am the one being written.

Story-tellers die and reincarnate,

the stories may change over time

but their telling remains.

Tears amass, but you give them weight.

When bodies cremate, ashes fall

the winds still carry them.

Introverted, I was quite quiet,

a child drowning in a world of opinions

not realizing the unique expressions

I am of all the Universes.

The man-made laws that govern this place

I know now, were created by words

that emerged from an air similar

to my own breath.

I embrace the disgrace

I bring upon my family's name

by not following in the footsteps

that were long since distorted,

by generations of men

walking over each other.

Scattered notes of a piano

accompanied by trumpet lines slithering across the room,

a slow Sunday afternoon.

Turning pages,

two come together

some words sound better, unread.

    -    the solution doesn't exist, and neither does the
         problem

To witness the Church's atrial architecture

I had to stretch my neck

and bend my knees.

The uneasiness I feel inside

in interactions with those I dislike

I know, are just reflections of me

I've yet to come to terms with

and I will.

I was on my way home

when I lost myself, now home.

Separated when young,

grew up not knowing who I really was

God's child, I saw God cry

when I was taken from Him.

He has waited endlessly since,

for the day I walk back

so He could tell me of the times

my tiny hands grasped His thumb,

and with one step forward,

how I slowly learned to stand up.

Don't you know that Jesus saved me?

Before Him,

I was so cynical.

He turned water into wine,

coke into lines, hope into signs

in addiction we were dying.

Look at me now,

a breathing miracle.

Not worthless, your tears are worth it

I know you're down

for life's not perfect.

In these oceans of highs and falls

unconditional love,

after every storm shall always resurface.

You are the fish and the river.

A new night,

against the darkness, the stars glitter above

like a shimmering black dress of diamonds.

Heights out of reach turn to

ladders of manifesting.

Once I was a rock,

now a mountain.

mokradi_

Thank you.

I am grateful for your attention. I am grateful for your time.

If you want to show further support, do consider leaving a review or reaching me directly with your feedback. It is humbling as always.

Until next time,

With love always,

mokradi

ISBN: 978-1-7776826-3-7

Concept by mokradi_

Illustrations and cover design by Tyler Dail

about the author/

mo-kra-di (they/his) is an indian storyteller and chronicler who focuses on themes of shared experience and collective memories with digital media as the primary platform for their artistic expression.

in the years to come, mokradi hopes to continue his digital exploration in themes of intersectional identities, transgenerational memories and mythologies through the in-between boundaries of prose and poetry.

Almost Satori follows mokradi's *Oja the Indian,* also available across select amazon platforms.
*@mokradi_*

Almost Satori accompanies illustrations by Tyler Dail.

Salt Lake City based artist, Tyler Dail, has been creating and selling art since 2010. He enjoys working with all mediums and techniques, especially black ink on white paper. The simplicity of lines are what he is most drawn to and yearns to dive deeper into. His art is constantly changing and taking on new personalities as he 'flows' through life.
@lucidmndof

about the book/

Almost Satori is a heart-stirring collection of poetry and prose rooted in themes of self-enquiry, intersectional identity and non-dual awareness.

through their poems, mokradi explores the co-existence of transgenerational memories and mythologies while also calling to attention the deep compassion of solitude in nature.

by drawing parallels to ongoing crises in social othering, climate change and collective trauma, mokradi invites readers to travel beyond their addictions to clinging, prejudice and opinions - often informed by self-centered ignorance.

accordingly, the terseness of the verses aim to capture the imagination of all Zen aficionados and poetry lovers - at the same time, inspiring readers to spark their own brilliant flashes of insight within the context of their lived experiences.